I have this little sister Lola.
She is small and very funny.
Lola's best, bestest friend Lotta has
come round to play...

characters created by lauren child

I will be
especially VERY
careful

Text based on the script

Illustrations from the TV animation

produced by Tiger Aspect

PUFFIN BOOKS
Published by the Penguin Group: London, New York, Australia,
Canada, India, Ireland, New Zealand and South Africa
Penguin Books Ltd, Registered Offices: 80 Strand, London WC2R 0RL, England

puffinbooks.com

First published 2008
Published in this edition 2012
004

Lotta has got a new c°a̱t and Lola REALLY likes it.

Lotta says,
"It's an extra special present from my granny.
She got it from a̱ᵇrо̱a̱d."

Lola says,
"It really is the most lо̱vе̱lie̱ṣt
thing I have EVER seen."

"It is very WHITE.
It reminds me of snow...

lovely

WHITE

snow.

And it is as

soft

as

feathers.

And...
as fluffy as a
baby kitten!"

In the kitchen, I say,
"Why are you wearing my mum's apron, Lotta?"

And Lola says,
"Because she is wearing her brand-new fluffy coat.
And she must
NOT do
spilling."

"How are you going
to keep it all new and
fluffy and WHITE, Lotta?"

And Lotta says...

"I will NOT get it wet in the rain.

I will **NOT** eat food, unless I am **VERY, VERY** careful.

And I will
NOT
play in the park
because of
the mud."

When it's time to go home, Lola says,
"We can do swapping if you like.
You can borrow my new clippy handbag...
and I could borrow
your fluffy coat!

And I will be especially VERY careful."

"Um... OK," says Lotta. "But you must
remember to keep it all
new and
fluffy and
WHITE."

But when Mum takes us to the supermarket, Lola says,

"HELP! The shopping trolley has got Lotta's coat!"

So I help Lola to untangle Lotta's coat from the shopping trolley.

PUFFA POPS

Lola says,
"Does it still
look like new?"

And I say,
"It's DEFINITELY
still brand-new."

In the post office, Lola says,
"Charlie, I'm just going to move
a little bit away from you because
you are sticky."

But then...

"Charlie...

Charlie!"

So I help to
un-stick Lola.

"Has it unstuck the
fluff?" asks Lola.

"Don't worry,
it's still all fluffy."

On the way to the library, Lola says,
"OH NO!
It's raining!
Lotta's coat is
getting all
WET."

And I say,
"Here,
have
Mum's
umbrella."

And Lola says,
"Is the coat
still fluffy
and WHITE?"

And I say,
"Yes, it's FINE."

"Phew!" says Lola. "It's DEFINITELY safe in the library, Charlie.

There is no rain in here and there are no shopping trolleys

and no sticky things...

But there are hundreds of books!"

On our way home,
I say,
"It's so sunny,
  I don't even
need my **coat**."

"Oh no! Lotta's coat!"

So we run back to the library,
but Lotta's coat is not anywhere.

"It's a dreadful
DISASTER, Charlie!"

At bedtime, Lola says,
"What am I going to say to Lotta?"

"You'll just have to tell her the truth...
that you lost her **coat**."

"But what if she doesn't LIKE
        me any more?" says Lola.

And I say,
        "I'm sure she will understand."

The next day,
    Lola sees Lotta
in the school playground.

"Hello, Lola!" says Lotta.
"Where's my
    fluffy coat?"

And Lola says

We went to the supermarket, and I kept it all fluffy...

I took it to the post office and it still looked like new...

And it rained, but I borrowed Mum's umbrella. And then we went to the library and...

"... It got **a bit,**
slightly LOST."

"But then you FOUND it?"
says Lotta.

And Lola says,
"No...
it is VERY lost.
I am extremely
VERY sorry, Lotta."

But just then Mini comes over.

"I've got
      your coat, Lola!
You left it in
      the library!"

And Lola and Lotta say,

"Oh, THANK YOU!"

In the classroom, Lola says,
"Oooh! That is a very fluffy WHITE pencil case.
Maybe I could borrow it?"
And Lotta says, "Mmm... no."